THIS BOOK BELONGS TO
kelcy west

HAPPY BIRTHDAY!
Love,

Nana

Published in the United States of America

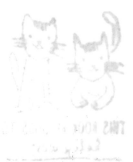

Preface

Every summer Aimee went to spend time with her 'Other Gs'. The 'Other Gs' are her bio dad's parents. Usually she and her cousins would all go spend a week during summer break there IT was a blast! Until the summer it all changed. Everyone was too busy to go the same week. Aimee just knew it was going to be b-o-r-i-n-g.

It wasn't that Aimee didn't love the Other Gs, she did! They loved her, too. She really liked spending time with them — going places and seeing her family was fun. She was just so used to having her cousins around when she was there, she could not imagine what it would be like being there without them.

That was the summer that Grandma got a puppy. Oh, what a puppy it was! It might have looked cute, all white, fluffy and small. Aimee thought it was adorable, but that puppy turned out to be the least boring thing of her summer that year.

Chapter 1

Mom was usually the one sitting on the bed as Aimee ran around the room pulling clothes and things to pack into the two bags she would take with her to her Other Gs. A week of summer break from school would normally be spent at the Other Gs with her cousins.

Not *this* year. This year, the week everyone could make it was not the same as anyone else's. Some had scout camps, sports camps, or extended family vacations. There was *no* way for everyone to be there the same week. This year, everyone was still going, but for a different week - boring.

Aimee sat on the bed to put the items her Mom was busy picking out for her to pack. This was not going to be fun. *What was there to do without her cousins?* That was the only thing on Aimee's mind.

There wasn't even going to be much time with her Uncle Tyler. He was going to be either working or taking college classes, plus he had football practice, too. There would be no one to play hide and seek with. No one to chase around the yard with squirt guns.

Sure the Other Gs would be willing, but they are, well . . . , *old*. They don't move fast; they are easy to catch. And Grumpa? He cheats at squirt guns! He uses the *hose*! That is all well and good when you have cousins to tag-team with. Someone distracts him while another sneaks up behind him with the hose from the back yard. But, when you are all by yourself? How can you be in two places at once?

Aimee listened to her mother talk about what fun she was going to have as they finished putting the last few items in the suitcase. "Really, Aimee, it won't be that bad."

"That's what you say."

The summer visit usually started out pretty boring. The drive there was long and hot. Aimee was always glad that Grumpa would start the car to blast the hot air out of the car with the air conditioner. That air definitely needed conditioning — otherwise Aimee would stick to the hot seat.

Aimee usually brought a book or video game to pass the time away in the backseat. This year, even that was different. Grandma was waiting for them at home. Aimee was now old enough, and tall enough to sit up front with a booster seat.

Aimee and Grumpa talked on the drive. They talked about school, cheerleading, Grumpa's garden and her Uncle Tyler. This time the drive didn't seem to take so long. It passed by faster than usual.

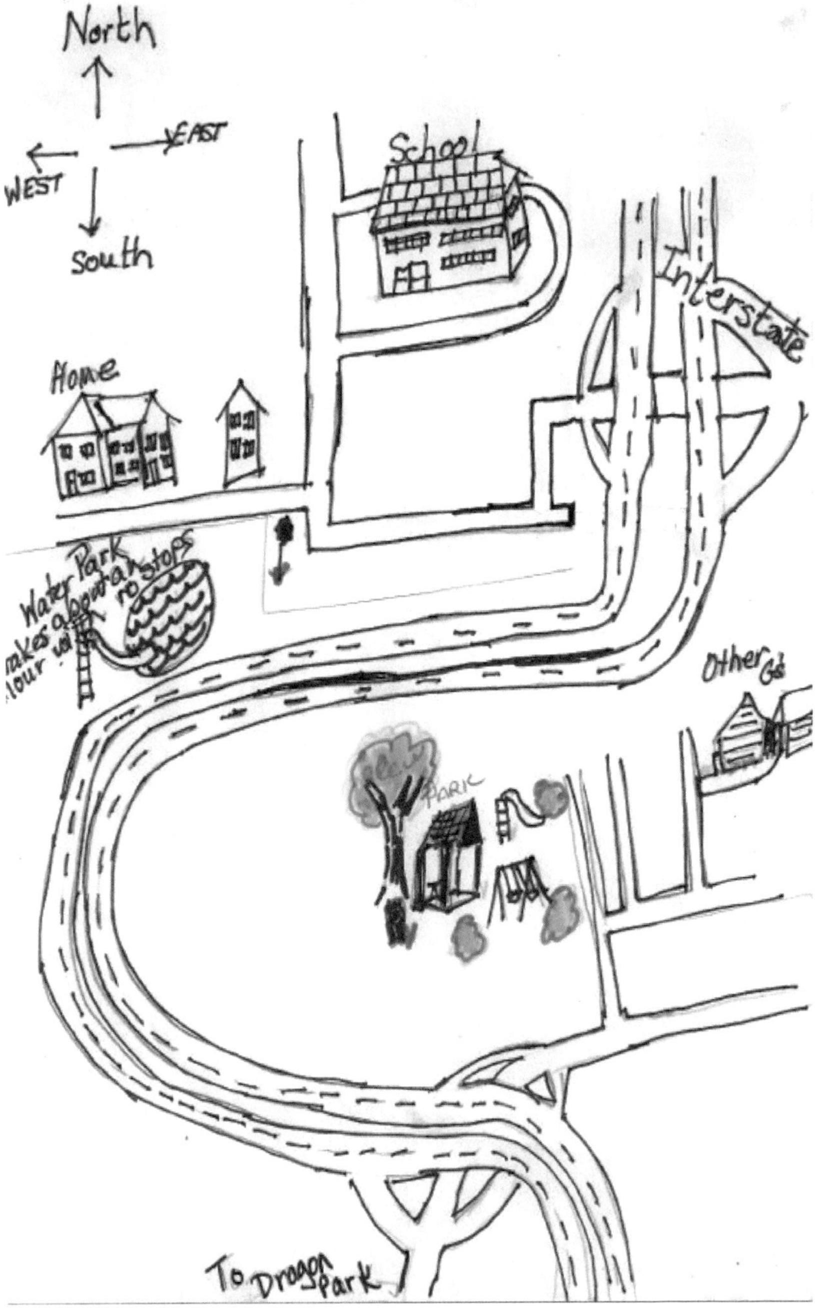
North
EAST
WEST
South
School
Interstate
Home
Water Park
Other G's
PARK
To Dragon Park

Chapter 2

The usual excitement and noise of their arrival was louder, even without her cousins. This time there was the added noise of a puppy barking. It was crazy. Aimee helped her Grandma catch the puppy and put it into the back yard, which was now fenced in. That was different, too.

The start of the visit and the end were always eventful. Arriving, there was so much catching up to do and settling in. After Grumpa brought in the bags, Grandma gave them a little snack. Aimee finished first and Grandma asked her to let the puppy back in the house.

"Sure!"

"Grandma, is it a boy or a girl?"

"Oh, it's a little girl puppy. I named her Snowball. We just call her Snow. Bet you can't guess *why*!"

"Um, because she is white!", Aimee giggled. Silly Grandma, that one was kind of obvious. Grandma's answer stopped Aimee in her path to the back door.

"No. Want to try again?"

"It's not because she's white?"

"No, that would be obvious, but that is not *why* she's named Snowball."

"Let me think." Aimee stood still for a minute or two, trying hard to think of another reason why the white furry puppy was named Snowball. She just couldn't think of another reason.

"Ok, Grandma, you are going to have to tell me. I can't figure it out."

"Well, you aren't completely wrong. Her being white has a bit to do with it. When Grumpa brought her home this past winter, there was snow on the ground. There she was all curled up in his hands. He came in the door and handed her to me. He said, 'Here'. I thought he was handing me a snowball."

"Grandma!"

Aimee shook her head and chuckled on the way to the back door. She was expecting to see the new little puppy sitting on the porch, eager to get back inside. When she swung the door open, the porch was empty. Concerned, Aimee stepped out onto the porch and looked around the yard calling out for the puppy.

"S-n-o-w! Snowball! Here Snow!" Aimee called out over and over. She ran out into the middle of the yard, searching for the puppy. She looked underneath the house through the crawl space that Grumpa had left open, no puppy. She went into the garage through the open side door; still no puppy.

Then she heard an excited bark. The puppy! It was coming from the *front* yard. Aimee carefully went through the gate and relocked it before running to the front yard.

Aimee came around the corner of the house to see the puppy barking and jumping at the front door. Aimee went to the porch and was on the first step before the puppy saw her.

Then the puppy jumped on her, as high as Aimee's knees. Aimee attempted to catch the puppy at first, but the puppy backed away and went back to jumping at the door again. The puppy ran back to Aimee and jumped on her knees again. Aimee felt the sweat from the heat and humidity run down her back and decided to just open the door and get them both inside to the air conditioning.

The puppy struggled to beat Aimee into the house and won! Grandma stood in the doorway between the living room and the kitchen with a confused look on her face. The yelping puppy jumped up into Grandma's arms as she bent to scoop up the puppy. Aimee shut the door, and flopped on the wood floor under the ceiling fan and right in front of the air conditioning vent.

"Where did y'all come from?"

Grandma moved to sit on the edge of the sofa with the puppy in her lap. She listened as Aimee told all about the search for Snowball. Snow licked Grandma and barked occasionally as if to put in her opinion as well.

Later that night Aimee's grandma asked if she was ready to read a story before bed. Each grandchild able to read, took a turn reading aloud most nights. Aimee was reading chapter books by herself now. First Aimee read a chapter and then Grandma.

When Grandma finished reading, she shut the bookmark between the pages and set the book on the dresser. At Aimee's feet lay a sleeping puppy.

"Well, missy, I think you have a bed buddy there."

"Grandma, can she stay?"

"Sure, if you don't mind. Snow doesn't."

Aimee grinned. Grandma had said the puppy liked to sleep with her and Grumpa. It made Aimee feel good to know that the puppy liked to sleep with her, too.

Grandma tucked Aimee in with a kiss on her forehead and lowered the dresser lamplight to a pale glow. Saying good night, she closed the door.

Snow was a sweet puppy. Aimee didn't want anything to happen to her. She *had* to find out how the puppy had gotten out of the yard.

Aimee lay still, trying not to disturb the sleeping puppy. Snow slept that first night curled up at Aimee's feet.

Chapter 3

The next morning, Grumpa was up early as usual, making breakfast. Aimee hopped onto a stool near the stove to have serious discussion. She was sure that Grumpa would help her.

"Grumpa, can I talk with you while you're making pancakes?"

"Sure, what about?"

"Did you know that Snow got out of the yard yesterday?"

"Aimee, Snow gets out of the yard a lot more often than just yesterday."

"She does? You mean this wasn't the first time?"

"No, it wasn't. I have walked the fence line trying to figure out where she is getting out. I haven't found it yet."

"I was going to ask you if there is a hole in the fence, or a low spot in the ground where she is crawling under the fence."

"No, no hole in the fence. I haven't found any low spots either."

"Are there any holes in the yard?"

"No, she isn't digging out either. I have to tell you, I am stumped, Aimee, plum stumped."

Aimee sighed. This was not the conversation she had imagined having with Grumpa last night before she fell asleep. No, this was not a simple problem at all.

"If I had time to just watch Snowball, maybe I could see where she is getting out. Things have been busy around here. Today I am taking Uncle Tyler to football practice and then his truck to the mechanic's. Do you want to come, too?"

"Grumpa, can I stay and watch the puppy for you?"

"Are you sure you don't want to go watch your Uncle Tyler at football practice?"

"I do, but can't I go do that another day? If I watch the puppy today, I might figure out where Snowball is getting out."

"That would be a big help. For now, let's get these pancakes ready and we can wake Uncle Tyler if he isn't up by the time they are all done."

Aimee helped Grumpa with breakfast. She set the table and handed him plates to fill with the yummy pancakes. By the time they were done, Tyler appeared sleepy eyed at the kitchen doorway.

"Do I smell pancakes?" Tyler's eyes were now wide open as he licked his lips, anxious for the pancakes.

After breakfast Grumpa left to take Tyler to practice. They wouldn't be back for hours. Aimee helped Grandma clean up from breakfast.

Aimee went outside with Grandma to help hang up laundry to dry. She tried to help Grandma hang the clothes, but the puppy kept jumping in the laundry basket. Aimee took the puppy off to a corner of the yard to play.

When Grandma was done, she walked over to where they were playing tug of war with an old piece of rope that Grumpa had knotted at each end for a puppy toy.

"Aimee, thank you for helping with the laundry. I am going to go clean the house, are you staying out here and playing with the puppy?"

"Grandma," Aimee sighed, "I didn't help with the laundry, I just played with the puppy so she wouldn't make *more* laundry."

Grandma laughed, "That *was* help! Thank you."

"You're welcome. I think we will stay out and maybe I can figure out how Snowball is getting out."

"I will bring you out a snack when I take a break from cleaning, ok?"

"Ok!"

At first Aimee and Snow played until the puppy got tired. Then Snow wandered off to lay in the shade. Aimee went to the patio and sat on the glider. Sliding back on the glider, Aimee made herself comfortable. *This is going to take a while*, she thought. If only she had brought a book out to read, but decided that she might forget to watch the puppy and then the opportunity would be lost.

The breeze was soft and the day was just warm enough, that soon Aimee began to feel sleepy. She shifted in the glider to a more comfortable position. Looking over to see if the movement had disturbed the puppy, but Snow was still asleep. As hard as she tried, Aimee could not keep her eyes open either. Soon she fell asleep, too.

Grandma looked out the kitchen window and saw in the shade of the tree - Aimee asleep on the glider, and at the base of the tree Snowball dozing also. Grandma decided that it was safe to start the pumpkin pie for Aimee. Surely the puppy would wake Aimee to play rather than escape.

Half an hour later, Aimee opened her eyes and yawned. *Oh, No!* Aimee looked over where the puppy had been sleeping under the tree. No puppy! She looked around the yard hoping to see the puppy. No puppy, the puppy was gone! She had fallen asleep and missed seeing the puppy escape.

Aimee started to stand up and walk around the yard, but her feet felt heavy. Looking down, there, on her feet was — the puppy! The puppy had not left the yard. Hmm, maybe Snowball only left the yard when she was alone.

Aimee wanted to share her discovery with Grumpa when he got home. The afternoon had not supplied as much information as she had hoped. They still didn't know where or how the puppy was getting out of the yard, but they did know she would stay when not alone.

Looking around the yard, Aimee thought about how they could keep an eye on Snow *and* leave the puppy alone in the yard at the same time. When Snowball woke up, Aimee walked the around the backyard fence, followed by the puppy. Aimee was looking beyond her Other Gs' yard. Could they hide in a neighbor's yard, she wondered?

Aimee would have to talk to Grumpa about asking the neighbors for permission to hide in their yards where Snowball couldn't see them. Then the puppy might think she was alone. This was going to take teamwork, a team of more than just two.

Grumpa and Tyler arrived home late in the afternoon. Uncle Tyler and Aimee gathered kindling for a bonfire after supper. Later that evening, Aimee enjoyed roasting marshmallows and catching fireflies, two of her favorite summer things to do.

The evening foe by quickly and Aimee forgot to tell Grumpa her idea to find out how Snowball was getting out of the fence. She and Snowball went to sleep curled up next to each other.

Chapter 4

The next morning Aimee woke to the barking of Snow. The frisky little puppy was yapping at Grumpa who was also late in waking up. He and Grandma had stayed up until the embers of the bonfire had burned out. Snow was used to breakfast being on time, so she was letting everyone know it was late. Aimee could hear the grumbling of Grumpa as he was getting up to go start coffee down the hall. Grandma was washing up the dirty cups of hot chocolate and marshmallow-crusted toasting sticks from last night. Aimee rushed over to Grandma.

"Gran, here, I will do that, I forgot about those!"

"No, Aimee, you and Tyler did your chores, this wasn't part of dinner, *this* was a treat. Besides I am almost done. Go set the table for breakfast. Maybe we could have cereal this morning?"

Grandma leaned down closer to Aimee's ear and whispered, "Make it easier on Grumpa, yes?"

Aimee grinned and nodded.

"I would love some cereal Grumpa!"

Grumpa just grumbled more. He liked making big breakfasts, but with the house emptying of children as they grew up, he only got to make the big breakfasts that he liked to eat when his grandchildren came to visit. He looked first at Aimee, then at Grandma, squinting his eyes.

"Now, you two know . . . "

He was interrupted by the pesky puppy and moved to silence the fur-ball so they didn't have to try to talk above the yapping.

Aimee grabbed the bowls and spoons from the counter setting the table quickly. She climbed on the kitchen stool, first resting her elbows on the table, then her chin on her hands to watch as Grumpa fed the disagreeable puppy. He put the bowl on the floor and the puppy was quiet, other than the sound of tiny teeth chomping on dry dog food.

"Now to *our* breakfast."

Grumpa moved to pull mixing bowls and measuring cups out. Aimee coughed to get Grandma's attention. Grandma turned to look at Aimee, who nodded at Grumpa and grinned, "What are we having?"

Grandma turned back to the sink, shaking her head and finished the last toasting stick. Drying her hands, Grandma walked over to Grumpa. Stretching up she kissed Grumpa's cheek, which made Aimee giggle.

"Grumpa, don't make a fuss. We were all up late last night. We aren't as picky as that puppy about when or what we eat this morning. Besides aren't we going to Dragon Park today?"

"Well, I am, I don't know what you two are doing. *If* you want to go with me, you best be ready when I am. Since little miss here has bowls out, I guess I could make some oatmeal."

Aimee rolled her eyes, leave it to Grumpa to make a big breakfast out of something quick like cereal.

"Momma, can you prep some fresh fruit to put in our oatmeal while I fry some bacon?" Grumpa lighted the gas flame under the iron skillet.

Grandma laughed and began cleaning and cutting up fruit, shaking her head again. Aimee watched her Other Gs make breakfast. It was nice. As they worked about the kitchen, they discussed with Aimee how the puppy could be getting out of the back yard.

During breakfast Aimee had told Grumpa about staying with Snowball and the puppy not trying to get out. She told him her idea to watch the puppy by hiding in the neighbors' yards. Grumpa wanted to check the fence one more time before they went to ask the neighbors about hiding behind and in their trees. He thought there had to be a spot he was missing that Snow could get out through.

After breakfast Grumpa and Aimee went out into the back yard. Grumpa went out the gate and around the house to the outside of the fence. Aimee walked around the inside to where Grumpa was. Aimee knelt down and pushed her hand against the fence.

"Aimee? What are you doing?"

"I am pushing on the fence like the puppy would do to get out."

Grumpa's head tilted to the side as he considered this. "I hadn't thought about that. You may just have something there. Hang on for a minute."

Grumpa went to the garage and dug around for a tennis ball. He went in the house and compared the size of the tennis ball with Snow's head. They were about the same size. Satisfied Aimee would have something to check the fence with, he went to find Aimee making a daisy chain from clover flowers in the grass where he left her.

"Think Grandma will like it?" Aimee looked up with a grin, a crown of clover flowers on her head. She had on a bracelet and a ring, both make of clovers. She gathered her flower jewelry and placed them on the shaded porch.

"You had time to make all that?"

"Yes, you were gone a while, Grumpa."

"I think she will like them just fine."

Grumpa handed Aimee the tennis ball, "Here, I measured this against the size of Snow's head. They are about the same size. That's the biggest part of her, if you can't find a way to poke that throughout the fence, she can't get out."

"Good idea!"

The two made their way around the fence from one end of the house, around the back to the garage. They even checked the gate between the house and the garage. No openings could be found that was large enough for the puppy to stick her head through. They had even tried pushing on the ground and gateposts to make a hole large enough for Aimee to push the ball outside the fence, but no place was found. They stood and shook their heads when they were done.

"Well, I think we deserve some ice cream, don't you, Aimee?"

"Aren't we going to Dragon Park?"

"Sure, we can get the ice cream on the way to the park. Maybe even on the way back."

"Think Grandma will let us get some both ways?"

"I don't know Aimee. If we eat all the picnic lunch she has packed for the park, I think she will."

Aimee took the tennis ball, putting it back in the box of outside toys Grumpa kept in the garage. Grumpa went in the house to see if Grandma was ready to get going to Dragon Park.

After getting home from Dragon Park, they were all tired. Since they stopped to eat dinner out on the way home, it was an early night, earlier than usual. It seemed like everyone was fast asleep the minute their heads hit the pillows, Snow included.

Chapter 5

The next morning Aimee woke and lay still with the puppy curled up asleep   resting its furry head on her shoulder. She thought about how else the puppy could be escaping.

The puppy yawned and walked over the covers on top of Aimee, causing her to giggle. Snow walked on top of Aimee's chest and licked her nose. She then sat down on Aimee's chest and licked her face clean. Aimee decided first they were going to have a talk.

"Snowball, I know you only get out of the yard because you don't like to be alone."

The puppy stood to get closer to Aimee's face, licking it again. Aimee sat up causing the puppy to roll off, but caught the rolling puppy. Aimee held the wiggling puppy in her lap.

"Snow you have to learn to stay *in* the fence. At least show me where you are getting out, so I can help Grumpa fix it."

Aimee gave up trying to hold and talk to the licking, squirmy Snow. Aimee got out of bed and headed off to the kitchen, the puppy following in hot pursuit. Grumpa fed the puppy and began to make breakfast with Aimee as his assistant once again.

This morning there were no yummy smells coming from the kitchen. Grumpa had bowls, spoons and boxes of cereal set out on the counter.

"Are we having cereal?"

"Yes, because as soon as you eat, we are using walkie-talkies and making a plan to stake out the back yard."

"What are walkie-talkies?"Aimee picked up the black and grey walkie-talkie Grumpa set in front of her,"Oh, I remember playing with Uncle Tyler with these when I was little."

"Well, we are going to use them to help figure out where we can watch the yard without Snow knowing about it. You stay inside the fence and see if you can see me. I talked to the neighbors this morning. We have permission for us to hide so we can watch the puppy. Grandma will put her in the yard so Snowball will think she is alone."

"We can see her, but she won't see us. Then we can see how she is getting out!"

"Exactly!"

Eating a quick breakfast, Aimee went to get dressed while Grumpa got his boots on and checked the batteries in the walkie-talkies. Grandma was up by then having her cup of coffee when Aimee came back to the kitchen.

"Sounds like you two have big plans this morning. How can I help?"

"Well, Grandma, once we have some places to hide, we will need you to put Snowball out in the back yard alone. We will watch until she gets out. Once she's out, we will have to get her back again. If all goes as planned Aimee and I can close off her escape route by tomorrow."

"How many places do you think we need to watch from Grumpa?"

"I am thinking three. What do you think Aimee?"

"Four? One person per side of the yard."

"If I am letting Snow out of the house, then I can watch out the kitchen window to the back yard. The corner by the end of the house, or the gate, are the only two places that I can't see from inside. "

"Well, Aimee, I don't think we need anyone eon the garage side. Besides, Snowball might hear someone in the garage and not try to get out. We need to find Tyler a spot out in front to of the gate, I think."

"Ok, so watching the side yard?"

"And the back part by where the garage and fence line meet."

Aimee went to stand in the back yard, while Grumpa went out the front door. First they checked where he could hide in the neighbor's yard that was beside the house. Grumpa shifted behind trees and shrubs, checking with Aimee on the walkie-talkie to see if she could see him. Grumpa decided the old oak tree was the best option next door. He would need to put his deer stand up against the tree to get high enough for the leaves to hide his body. Aimee took a snack break while Grumpa went to get permission from the neighbor to put up the deer stand.

"Well, how goes the stake out?"

"We are still just planning the stake out Grandma, we aren't staking anything yet."

"Ok, so how goes the planning of the stake out?"

"Grumpa is asking permission to put his deer stand up in Mr. Roy's yard. Then we have to figure out where in Miss Michie's yard I will hide."

"Snack?"

"That's what I am here for Grandma!"

Grandma fixed Aimee a sandwich and a glass of milk. By the time she was done, Grumpa was coming in the front door. Grandma had Aimee put water in her empty milk glass so the milk residue wouldn't dry on the bottom while she made Grumpa a sandwich.

After the break Grump and Aimee checked where she could hide in Miss Michie's yard. There weren't as many trees and they were younger trees, so the limbs were lower to the ground. Miss Michie came out to talk to Grumpa while he and Aimee radioed back and forth. Miss Michie said she would be able to help Aimee get in and out of the tree. They found a maple with a limb just above Aimee's head that would be perfect for her to sit on. Grumpa hopped up on it to check; it held his weight just fine. Other than his long dangling legs, Aimee couldn't see him.

The last place to hide would be where Tyler would hide on the other side of the garage gate. Grumpa and Aimee met in front of the garage gate. Looking out from the gate, there was no where to hide. The other side of the street was a vacant lot. Across the next street over was a park. The nearest place to hide in the park was too far to see well even with the binoculars, the view looking back wouldn't be any better.

"I don't know how we are going to manage this side."

"Well, someone could hide in a car."

"Snow might see them, Aimee."

"Not if they hide in the car and use the side mirror to look out."

"Aimee! How did you come up with that?"

"Playing hide and seek. I hid in the back seat of the car and looked out using the side mirror to see where Grandma was one time."

"Well, if Tyler backed the car in, he could sit in the front seat and use the mirror to see the gate, but Snow wouldn't see him."

With the positions settled, Grumpa and Aimee prepared for the next day. Aimee helped with setting up the deer stand. When Uncle Tyler came home from practice he was filled in on the plans.

After supper that night they helped Grandma prepare a cook out the next day. Cookies were mixed and baked. Homemade ice cream was made; samples were taste tested to make sure it would be just right.

Grampa

Aimee

Uncle Tyler

PARK

Chapter 6

The next morning when Aimee awoke, she slipped her feet out from underneath the sleeping puppy's head, carful not to wake Snow. Aimee went to the kitchen and was startled to find Grandma sitting at the kitchen table drinking coffee.

"Grandma, what are you doing up so early?"

"Early? You mean late? I couldn't sleep last night. I tried reading, but I finished my book. Then I got up and made the caramel French toast that Grumpa likes so much. It's the only breakfast that I can make before he can."

"The *only*?"

"The only, want to know my secret?"

"Sure!"

"I make it the night before."

They both laughed out loud at first, then shushed and giggled. Grumpa and Tyler were still sleeping, along with the puppy.

"I put it all together and put in the fridge. Then, I set it out in the morning while the coffee is making and the oven is heating up. Pop it in the oven and it is done."

Aimee giggled. It *was* hard to beat Grumpa getting up in the morning. That was just a Grumpa fact. She understood the only way Grandma could make breakfast that would beat Grumpa, was one she made ahead of time.

"Breakfast will be ready, by the way, in about fifteen minutes."

"What time will Uncle Tyler get up?"

"Probably right before lunch. Then we'll grill out. After lunch you, Grumpa and Tyler go for a walk. Snow and I will clean up from lunch giving everyone time to set up. When I get the signal, I'll put Snow outside."

"Did Grumpa talk to Uncle Tyler last night?"

"Yes, and Tyler backed my car in the driveway, so he can sit in the front seat and use the side view mirror to watch the gate."

"I hope he doesn't shut the door so loud that Snow knows he's in there."

"I am sure he won't."

Aimee was all smiles. She was so excited to know before the end of her stay, that Grandma's puppy would be safe. She had enjoyed her furry bed buddy.

After Grandma's breakfast, Aimee helped Grandma get ready for the cook out at lunch. Uncle Tyler picked up the yard and moved lawn furniture so they could play a game of washers while waiting on the food to grill.

Aimee and Grandma took glasses of iced tea out to the shade of the glider in the back yard. While they sat gliding back and forth, Aimee and Grandma talked. Aimee was worried about the safety of the puppy after she left, she hoped they would find and fix how Snow was getting out of the fence.   Aimee, enjoyed the puppy following her everywhere, she would miss that.

Grumpa and Tyler took out three walkie-talkies for each of them to use in the stake out later, along with binoculars and the burgers and hot dogs to grill. Tyler put the stake out items on the picnic table and Grumpa took the meat to the grill. After eating they played a round robin tournament of washers, then had ice cream for dessert.

By three o'clock, everyone was getting ready to go to his or her hiding place. Uncle Tyler went to hide in Grandma's car as planned. Grumpa and Aimee walked to the neighbors' yard, where silently they waved to each other as Grumpa stopped to climb the deer stand up into the oak tree, and Aimee continued down the hill to the maple in the yard behind her grandparents.

Walking down the hill, so many thoughts were on Aimee's mind — whether or not she would have trouble climbing into the tree, dropping the binoculars, and wondering if she would fall out of the tree. It was a little scary.

Once she was in the yard, Aimee saw that through Miss Michie's kitchen window, the gray headed lady was waving. Aimee waved back. It warmed her heart to know that so many people were helping.

Miss Michie had been worried about Aimee climbing the tree, so, she had pulled her stepladder out of her storage shed and set it up next to the tree so Aimee could use it to get up in to the tree safely.

Now standing at the tree in the yard by herself, Aimee wasn't as scared as she had been walking down the hill. She saw Miss Michie was there to help if she needed it. She could do this.

Aimee had seen where a branch had broken off and stuck out from the trunk above the limb she planned to sit. She swung the binoculars up and over her head, letting the strap fly, catching on the broken off piece — just like a hook. Now she would have both hands free to climb. She put the walkie talkie on the stepladder, with a backward glance to Miss Michie, and got a thumbs up. Aimee couldn't see Miss Michie as well once perched on the branch. She could just see the top of the nice lady's head. That little bit of reassurance was just the boost to her confidence Aimee needed. She was a go. Grabbing the walkie-talkie off the ladder below and behind her, she turned it on. Aimee could hear her Grumpa calling for her in a frantic voice, and then heard a phone ring before she could hit the mike button. Over the walkie talkie came Grumpa's voice.

"Hello . . . Michie? . . . Oh, yes. . . . . Ok, thank you. No, I haven't heard from her yet, but . . ."

Then silence.

Now Aimee pushed the button like Grumpa had reminded her . "Aimee in position." And let go of the button.

"Aimee! I got worried when you didn't respond as you were walking down the hill. Miss Michie said you were set, and to remind you to just shake a limb and she will come out and help you."

"It's ok. I forgot to turn on the walkie talkie until I was set up, but I am ready now."

It was a second before Aimee realized she hadn't let up on the button. She thought, '*I have to remember that.*'

Aimee raised the binoculars to her eyes and adjusted them as Grumpa had shown her yesterday afternoon at the park, so that she could see the yard.

Then she heard Grumpa from the walkie talkie, "I am going to give Grandma the signal."

Grumpa texted Grandma, and in a few minutes Aimee saw her shooing the puppy out from the back door. The puppy first stood at the back door, and then jumped at the door. A few barks later, the puppy was becoming bored with being ignored and began to wander the yard. Aimee knew from past experience that the puppy wouldn't stay alone for long in the yard. She leaned forward a little on the limb and reached her arm around the trunk of the tree to steady herself while holding the binoculars in her other hand.

The puppy went toward Grumpa, at Aimee's right. She went to the fence and put her front paws up on it. Aimee held her breath. The puppy's ears were perked up. Aimee was afraid Snow had spotted Grumpa. A few seconds later, though it felt like hours to Aimee, the puppy walked toward Aimee. The puppy sniffed the back fence row from the corner between Aimee and Grumpa over to the garage. Snowball then darted to the porch steps and stopped with her front paws back on the door barking. Aimee grinned. Grandma must have made some noise that made Snow think she was coming to let her in. After barking a bit, Snow came back down the steps into the grass, then over to the gate between the garage and house.

First Snow put her paws on the gate, as she had down on the side fence in front of Grumpa. The puppy barked a little, then got down and ran back on the porch again, as if she was expecting Grandma to let her in. Grandma didn't come, so once more Snowball went back to the gate. This time

Aimee's mouth dropped open. She could not believe what she saw the puppy do!

The puppy began pawing at the white plastic lattice piece Grumpa had attached to the lower part of the gate with zip ties. It overlapped the bottom of the gate and the gate posts, hanging a couple of inches and grazed the ground when the gate was swung open. Grumpa had put it there to cover the gape between the gate and ground. The puppy pawed at the plastic, catching her paw in the lattice holes and pulled back. The plastic lattice bent, Snow ducked her head to get between lattice and the ground. It took a few tries before her timing was perfect, but then the puppy head was between the gate frame and the ground. Snow dropped her body to the ground and scooted under the plastic and gate.

Aimee let out a yelp! She was stunned. She never thought about Snowball being able to pull something back. She bet Grumpa hadn't either. The walkie talkie clicked and Uncle Tyler's voice boomed.

"Got Snowball! Did you guys see that?"

Aimee took a deep breath and waited a second before pushing her mike button.

"I did! I saw the whole thing! She pulled the plastic back with her paw and crawled under."

"Good to know I wasn't the only one, Aimee!" Uncle Tyler's voice sounded as amazed as Aimee felt.

Aimee turned to hook her binoculars back up on the tree trunk and climb down. As she was turning to grab the trunk, there was Miss Michie beside the stepladder. Miss Michie had a pair of binoculars hanging from her neck.

"Did you see that Aimee? Well, I never would have thought of that, did you? Did your grandparents see it?"

"I don't know"

"Well, I saw, and when she started pulling at the plastic on the fence I was in the bathroom standing in my tub, I got there just in time to see her run into your uncle's hands, did you see that?"

"No, I could only see the gate. Really? Uncle Tyler caught her?"

"Yes, he must have gotten out of the car when he realized what she was doing."

Miss Michie held the stepladder steady while Aimee climbed on, reaching back into the tree for the binoculars and set them on the top alongside the walkie talkie. She climbed down and Miss Michie handed her the binoculars and radio. Aimee thanked Miss Michie and ran to meet her Grumpa who had climbed out of his tree stand.

By the time they were back at the house, Grandma and Uncle Tyler were in the house, sitting at the kitchen table with glasses of lemonade. There were glasses of the cold drink sitting in wait for Grumpa and Aimee.

Much laughter and retelling of Snowball's last escape were told from all views. Grandma had gone to the living room window and pulled the couch out from under the driveway window and stood at it to see the gate. She looked down to see Snowball wiggle out. Grandma said she didn't see Tyler get out of her car, but he was just there when Snow ran into his hands.

Uncle Tyler's version was about deciding to get out of the car to watch and catch her. He said Grandma's moving the couch inside must have distracted Snowball from seeing him get out of the car. He was on the far side of the car when she came back to start pulling at the lattice and was able to get in front of the gate just as she freed herself.

"I was trying to get to her before she was loose."

Uncle Tyler and Grumpa moved dirt from the side yard to build up the ground under the gate.   Then they placed concrete stepping stones onto the dirt so Snowball couldn't dig under the gate, and removed the gap that the plastic lattice didn't really fill.

After dinner, they all sat in the front yard eating ice cream. This time Grandma put Snow in the back yard by herself. There was no plastic lattice to bend, only hard concrete and gate. Snowball did try to move them before giving up and sitting down to wait until someone let her out.

Snowball was safe at last.

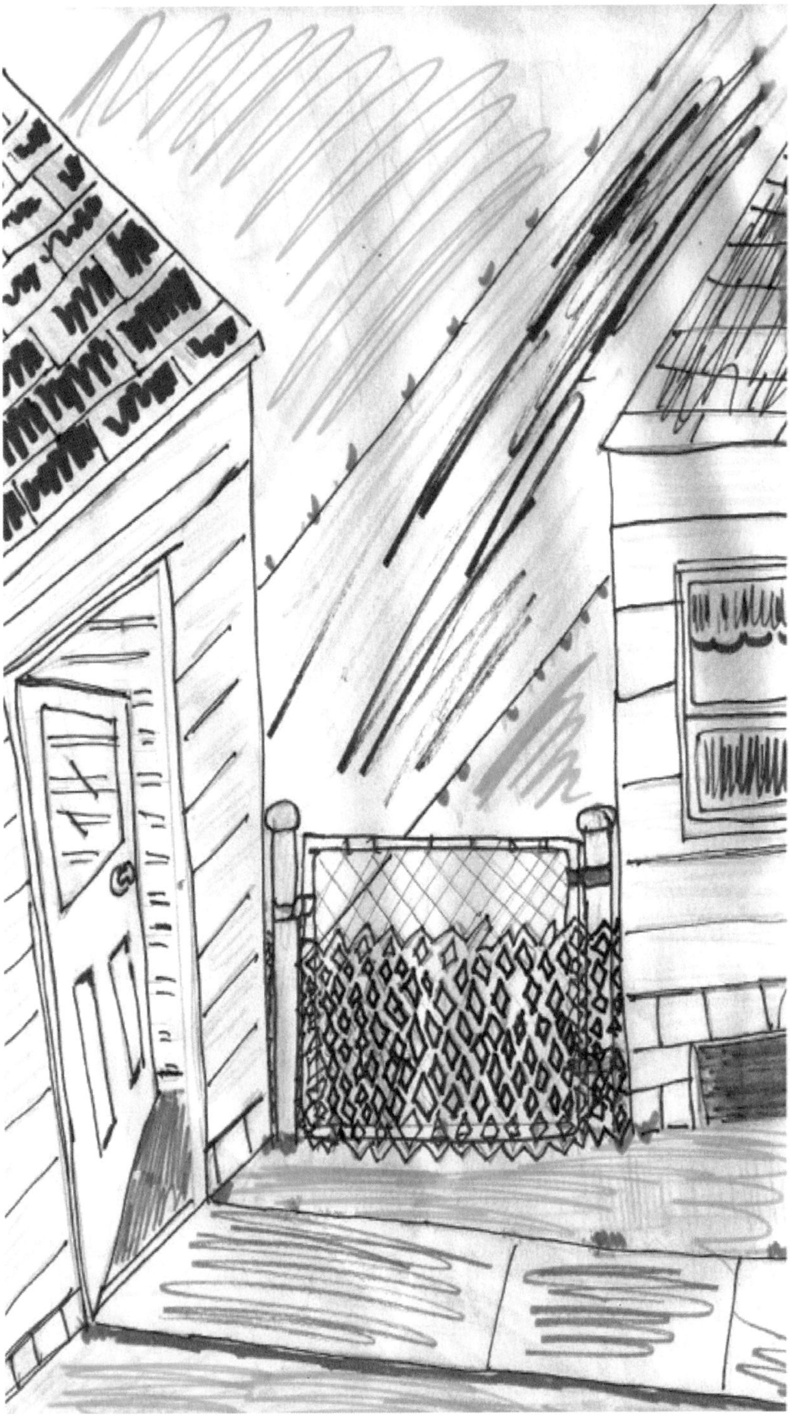

ACKNOWLEDGEMENTS

I want to thank my long time friend and editor, Lisa Stallings, without her 'red pencil' and helpful comments and questions this story would have never been completed. Also to Miss Vivie for the confidence boost and help with the last rewrite. Natalie Stanfield Thomas, who kept me feed with coffee and stuffed French toast whenever my muse waned, as well as encouragement, thank you. My biggest cheerleader, Marcy Bierman, she helps me keep my ego fueled.

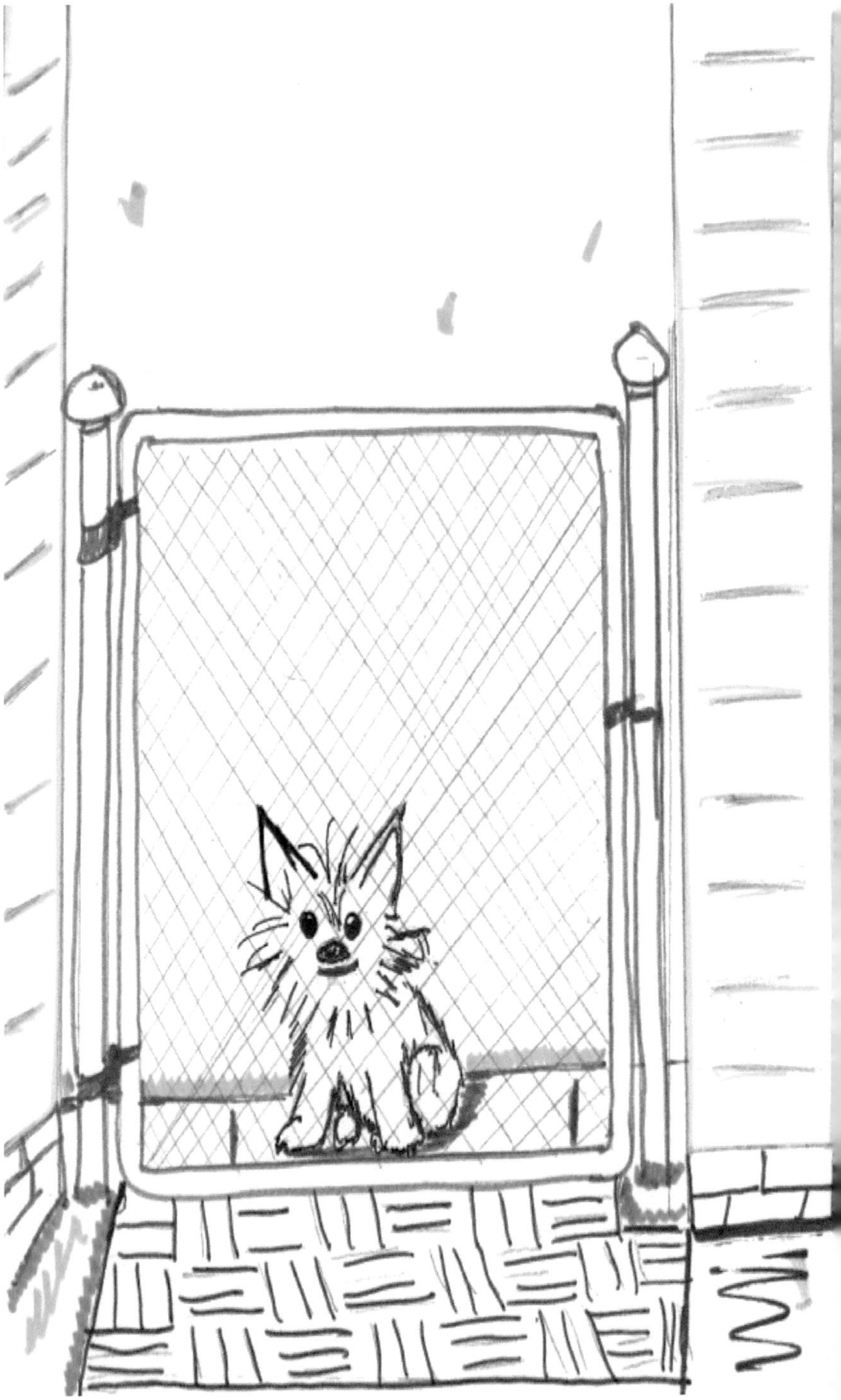

.

Made in the USA
Middletown, DE
23 December 2017